BLOOMSBURY CHILDREN'S BOOKS
Bloomsbury Publishing Plc
50 Bedford Square, London, WC1B 3DP, UK

BLOOMSBURY, BLOOMSBURY CHILDREN'S BOOKS and the Diana logo are trademarks of Bloomsbury Publishing Plc

First published in Great Britain 2018 by Bloomsbury Publishing Plc

Text by Teresa Heapy
Illustrations by Artful Doodlers based on an original style developed by Lucy Fleming
Text and illustrations copyright © Bloomsbury Publishing Plc 2018

A catalogue record for this book is available from the British Library

ISBN: PB: 978 1 4088 9685 3; eBook: 978 1 4088 9686 0

2 4 6 8 10 9 7 5 3 1

Printed in China by Leo Paper Products, Heshan, Guangdong

All papers used by Bloomsbury Publishing Plc are natural, recyclable products from
wood grown in well managed forests. The manufacturing processes conform to
the environmental regulations of the country of origin.

To find out more about our authors and books visit www.bloomsbury.com and sign up for our newsletters

Princess Snowbelle

and the Snow Games

Libby Frost

BLOOMSBURY
CHILDREN'S BOOKS
LONDON OXFORD NEW YORK NEW DELHI SYDNEY

Snowbelle, Princess of Frostovia,
was with her brothers Nicholas and Noel
by the frozen Opaline Lake.
She was waiting for her friend Sparkleshine.

It was the day of the Snow Games,
an annual contest between the kingdoms
of Frostovia and Snowland.
Sparkleshine's brothers, Jonathan and James
were competing too.

"I can't wait for the Games to start!" Snowbelle said excitedly.
"I do hope we win the Ice Trophy this time!"
"I'm going to win the sledging race for sure!" replied Noel with a cheeky grin.
"I've fitted my sledge with extra-fast runners. NO ONE can beat me!"
"Well I'm definitely winning the running race,"
said Nicholas, doing his warm-ups.
"I've been training for weeks."

Just then Snowbelle's mother and father came back
from twirling on the icy lake.

"Now, children," they said.
"Remember, it's not about winning,
it's about trying your best."

The Frostovian children grinned at each other.
They wanted to WIN that trophy!

When the royal family of Snowland arrived,
the two families greeted each other.

Snowbelle gave Sparkleshine a big hug.
"It's so good to see you!" she said.

"And now," said Snowbelle's father,
"let the Snow Games begin!"

The first race was sledging – from the top of the hill, to the very bottom.

Noel took off fast . . .

Too fast!
His super-speedy runners
sent his sledge spinning out of control
and he tumbled over in a heap of snow.

James won the race!

"Bad luck, Noel," said James.
"Better luck next time!" Nicholas joked as he limbered up for the running race.

"It's twice round the lake," called Snowbelle's mother.
"Ready . . . steady . . . GO!"

Nicholas ran like the wind
and finished two laps before
the others had finished even one!

"Well done, Nicholas!" cried Snowbelle.
"Now it's one all!"

"Yes, well done!"
Jonathan added.

The third event was a horse race through the forest
for Snowbelle and Sparkleshine.

Snowbelle and her white horse, Icetail, lined up next to Sparkleshine.
Sparkleshine was riding Crystalmane,
her piebald horse with a beautiful glittery mane.

"Are you ready?" called Snowbelle's father. "On your marks . . . get set . . . GO!"

"Come on, Icetail!" cried Snowbelle.
"We can do it!"

The horses set off at a gallop, sending up flurries of snow.
Sparkleshine raced ahead.
Snowbelle clung on tightly as Icetail dodged through the trees.

Then suddenly . . .

Disaster!

Snowbelle's velvet cape got caught on a low-hanging branch.
She couldn't move!

Sparkleshine and Crystalmane disappeared into the distance.

"OH NO!" Snowbelle cried.
"We'll never win the race now, Icetail!"

But then she heard the pounding of hooves.
Sparkleshine was racing back to **rescue** her!

"I couldn't leave my **best friend** behind!" said Sparkleshine.
"Hold steady!" She carefully unhooked the cape, and soon Snowbelle was **free**.

"But you would have won the race—" began Snowbelle.
"Let's finish it together!" said Sparkleshine.

"You're the best friend ever," said Snowbelle,
as they crossed the finish-line holding hands.

Everyone was glad to see the girls back safe.
"We were worried about you two!" said Noel.

The horse race was declared a draw, so now the winner of the Snow Sculpture contest would win the Ice Trophy for their family.

But Snowbelle looked at her friend, and remembered how Sparkeshine's kindness had meant that she lost the race.

SNOW GAMES

Sledging 🛡 Snowland

Running 👑 Frostovia

"It doesn't matter who wins!" she blurted out.
"Let's all work together and make the best snow sculpture ever!"
"That's a great idea!" said Nicholas.

And so the children worked as a team to make a magical snow palace.

It had lots of tiny windows and a huge door with a drawbridge.
It was topped with tall towers and delicate, icy turrets.

The children stood back to admire their work.
"It's beautiful," breathed Snowbelle.

The Kings and Queens of Snowland and Frostovia turned to their children.

"Your snow sculpture is magnificent!" they said.
"We are very proud of you working together as a team – and the Ice Trophy is yours to share."

They all cheered as Snowbelle's mother picked up the glittering cup.
It was made entirely of ice and decorated with tiny, shining snowflakes.

Noel rushed over to his mother. "Can I hold it?" he asked.

But in his excitement, he knocked
the trophy from her hands and it
shattered on the cold, hard ground.

Everyone gasped in horror.
"Oh no!" said Noel. "I'm sorry!"

But Snowbelle had an idea.
"Don't worry!" she said. "I can use my magic bracelet!"

She shook the delicate silver charm, once . . . twice . . .
and suddenly, with a little chime of bells . . .

the Ice Trophy was whole again!

The children hugged each other.
"And now, I think we all deserve a treat!" announced Snowbelle's father.

The spectators came to join in the celebrations
and the Palace Cook appeared with trays of buttered crumpets
and cups of steaming hot chocolate.

"Don't forget the trophy," smiled Snowbelle's mother.
"You hold it with me, dear Sparkleshine," said Snowbelle,
as they lifted the cup high.

"This belongs to ALL of us!"